Kangaroo didn't like the way she looked,
with her short stumpy legs
and her even shorter, stumpier tail.

One day, Kangaroo shouted to the gods,
"Will you make me look different?"

Why the Kangaroo Jumps

by Rudyard Kipling

Retold by Rob Lloyd Jones

Illustrated by John Joven

Long, long ago, in a dry dusty desert,
the first kangaroo sat on a rock
and grumbled.

All day, Kangaroo grumbled and
moaned and grunted and groaned.

The gods refused, so Kangaroo kept yelling.
"All right then!" one of them finally agreed.

The gods flew to a wild dog,
who was snoozing in the shade.
"Wake up," they ordered.
"Make Kangaroo different!"

The dog sat up and smiled a wicked smile. His beady eyes glinted and his sharp teeth gleamed in the sunlight.

And then...

YAAA!

Kangaroo leaped
from her rock
and ran.

Wailing and whimpering, Kangaroo fled
from the wild dog. The wild dog chased her
over sun-baked rocks and across the
sun-scorched desert.

He chased her between
towering mountains.

He chased her through long wavy grass
and short scratchy grass.

He chased her all the way across the desert
until Kangaroo reached...

...a river!

Kangaroo stared at the opposite bank.
"I can't swim!" she gasped. "How will I get across?"

There was **only** one thing to do...

Kangaroo crouched
down low on her
short stumpy legs...
AND
SHE
JUMPED!

In one great bound,
she leaped right
across the river.

The wild dog kept chasing, and Kangaroo kept jumping. As she jumped, her back legs grew big and strong, and her tail grew fat and long.

She jumped between trees and over the river,
back across the desert to where she began.

Then she yelled to the gods high in the sky.

"Why did you make that wicked dog chase me?"

WHY?

"You wanted to be different,"
one of the gods replied.

"Now you are."

Kangaroo had been tricked, but the more she thought about it, the less she minded.

In fact, she realized she was happy.

After all, jumping was
rather fun.

'Why the Kangaroo Jumps' is from the book
'Just So Stories' by Rudyard Kipling,
which tells stories of how animals
came to be the way they are.

Edited by Lesley Sims
Designed by Laura Nelson Norris

First published in 2018 by Usborne Publishing Ltd., Usborne House, 83-85 Saffron Hill,
London EC1N 8RT, England. www.usborne.com Copyright © 2018 Usborne Publishing Ltd.